WALT DISNEY'S MOTHER GOOSE

Illustrations by the Walt Disney Studio
Adapted by Al Dempster

A GOLDEN BOOK • NEW YORK

 Published in the United States by Golden Books, an imprint of Random House Children's Books, a division of Random House, Inc., New York, and simultaneously in Canada by Random House of Canada Limited, Toronto, in conjunction with Disney Enterprises, Inc. Originally published in 1949 in slightly different form by Golden Books.

Library of Congress Control Number: 2004100451
ISBN: 0-7364-2310-9
www.goldenbooks.com
Printed in the United States of America
First Random House Edition 2004 30 29 28 27 26 25 24

THE QUEEN OF HEARTS

The queen of hearts,
She made some tarts,
All on a summer's day.
The knave of hearts,
He stole those tarts,
And with them ran away.

The king of hearts
Called for those tarts,
And beat the knave full sore;
The knave of hearts
Brought back those tarts,
And said he'd steal no more.

HEY, DIDDLE, DIDDLE

Hey, diddle, diddle, the cat and the fiddle,
The cow jumped over the moon;
The little dog laughed to see such sport,
And the dish ran away with the spoon.

CROSS PATCH

Cross patch,
Draw the latch,
Sit by the fire and spin;
Take a cup
And drink it up,
And call your neighbors in.

LITTLE JACK HORNER

Little Jack Horner sat in a corner,
Eating a Christmas pie;
He put in his thumb, and took out a plum,
And said, "What a good boy am I!"

JACK SPRAT

Jack Sprat could eat no fat,
His wife could eat no lean;
And so betwixt them both, you see,
They licked the platter clean.

LITTLE BETTY BLUE

Little Betty Blue
    Lost her holiday shoe.
What shall little Betty do?
    Buy her another
To match the other,
    And then she'll walk in two.

JUMPING JOAN

Here am I, little Jumping Joan.
When nobody's with me,
I'm always alone.

DEEDLE, DEEDLE DUMPLING

Deedle, deedle dumpling, my son John,
Went to bed with his stockings on;
One shoe off and one shoe on,
Deedle, deedle dumpling, my son John.

THIS LITTLE PIG

This little pig went to market,
This little pig stayed at home,
This little pig had roast beef,
This little pig had none,
This little pig cried, "Wee-wee-wee!"
All the way home.

MARY'S LAMB

Mary had a little lamb,
Its fleece was white as snow;
And everywhere that Mary went,
The lamb was sure to go.

It followed her to school one day,
Which was against the rule;
It made the children laugh and play
To see a lamb at school.

ONE TO TEN

1, 2, 3, 4, 5,
I caught a hare alive;
6, 7, 8, 9, 10,
I let him go again.

JACK BE NIMBLE

Jack be nimble,
Jack be quick,
Jack jump over
The candlestick.

PETER, PETER, PUMPKIN EATER

Peter, Peter, pumpkin eater,
Had a wife and couldn't keep her;
He put her in a pumpkin shell,
And there he kept her very well.

Handy Pandy, Jack-a-dandy,
Loved plum cake and sugar candy;
He bought some at a grocer's shop,
And out he came, hop, hop, hop.

THIS IS THE WAY THE LADIES RIDE

This is the way the ladies ride:
Trot, trot! Trot, trot! Trot, trot!

This is the way the gentlemen ride:
Gallop-a-trot! Gallop-a-trot!

This is the way the farmers ride:
Hobbledy-hoy! Hobbledy-hoy!

SIMPLE SIMON

Simple Simon met a pieman,
Going to the fair;
Says Simple Simon to the pieman,
"Let me taste your ware."

Says the pieman to Simple Simon,
"Show me first your penny."
Says Simple Simon to the pieman,
"Indeed I have not any."

He went to catch a dickey-bird,
And thought he could not fail,
Because he'd got a little salt
To put upon his tail.

Simple Simon went a-fishing,
For to catch a whale;
All the water he had got
Was in his mother's pail.

He went for water in a sieve,
But soon it all ran through;
And now poor Simple Simon
Bids you all adieu.

DING, DONG, BELL

Ding, dong, bell,
Pussy's in the well!
Who put her in?—
Little Johnny Green.
Who pulled her out?—
Big Johnny Stout.
What a naughty boy was that
To try to drown poor pussy cat,
Who never did him any harm,
But killed the mice in his father's barn.

A DILLAR, A DOLLAR

A dillar, a dollar,
A ten o'clock scholar,
What makes you come so soon?
You used to come at ten o'clock,
And now you come at noon.

BOBBY SHAFTOE

Bobby Shaftoe's gone to sea,
Silver buckles at his knee;
He'll come back and marry me,—
Pretty Bobby Shaftoe!

THERE WERE TWO BLACKBIRDS

There were two blackbirds,
Sitting on a hill,
The one named Jack,
The other named Jill.

Fly away, Jack!
Fly away, Jill!
Come again, Jack!
Come again, Jill!

OLD KING COLE

Old King Cole was a merry old soul,
And a merry old soul was he;
He called for his pipes and he called for his bowl,
And he called for his fiddlers three!

Humpty Dumpty sat on a wall,
Humpty Dumpty had a great fall;
All the King's horses and all the King's men
Couldn't put Humpty Dumpty together again.

THE OLD WOMAN WHO LIVED IN A SHOE

There was an old woman who lived in a shoe;
She had so many children she didn't know what to do.
She gave them some broth, without any bread;
She hugged them and kissed them and sent them to bed.

ROCK-A-BYE, BABY

Rock-a-bye, baby,
On the tree top!
When the wind blows,
The cradle will rock;
When the bough breaks,
The cradle will fall;
Down will come baby,
Cradle and all.

RUB A DUB DUB

Rub a dub dub,
Three men in a tub,
And who do you think they be?
The butcher, the baker,
The candlestick maker.
Turn 'em out, knaves all three.

JACK AND JILL

Jack and Jill went up the hill
To fetch a pail of water.
Jack fell down and broke his crown
And Jill came tumbling after.

Up Jack got, and home did trot
As fast as he could caper,
Went to bed and plastered his head
With vinegar and brown paper.

LITTLE MISS MUFFET

Little Miss Muffet
Sat on a tuffet,
Eating her curds and whey.
There came a great spider,
And sat down beside her,
And frightened Miss Muffet away!

HICKORY, DICKORY, DOCK

Hickory, dickory, dock,
The mouse ran up the clock.
  The clock struck one,
  The mouse ran down;
Hickory, dickory, dock.

LITTLE TOMMY TUCKER

Little Tommy Tucker
Sings for his supper.
What shall he eat?
White bread and butter.

How shall he cut it
Without e'er a knife?
How shall he marry
Without any wife?

GEORGIE PORGIE

Georgie Porgie, pudding and pie,
Kissed the girls and made them cry.
When the boys came out to play
Georgie Porgie ran away.

WEE WILLIE WINKIE

Wee Willie Winkie runs through the town,
Upstairs and downstairs, in his nightgown;
Rapping at the window, crying at the lock,
"Are the babies in their beds, for now it's eight o'clock!"

BYE, BABY BUNTING

Bye, baby bunting,
Daddy's gone a-hunting,
To get a little rabbit's skin
To wrap the baby bunting in.